# The Luminous Pearl

# The Luminous Pearl

## A CHINESE FOLKTALE

Retold by **Betty L. Torre**

Illustrated by **Carol Inouye**

Orchard Books

New York

Orchard Books
A division of Franklin Watts, Inc.
387 Park Avenue South
New York, NY 10016

Manufactured in the United States of America
Printed by General Offset Company, Inc.
Bound by Horowitz/Rae
Book design by Carol Inouye
Typography by High Resolution, Inc.
10   9   8   7   6   5   4   3   2   1
The text of this book is set in 15 pt. ITC Garamond Light
The illustrations are executed in watercolor and gouche.


This story is adapted from "The Pearl That Shone by Night,"
from *Favourite Folktales of China*. Translated by John Minford.
Beijing, China: New World Press, 1983.


Library of Congress Cataloging-in-Publication Data

Torre, Betty L.
      The luminous pearl : a Chinese folktale / retold by Betty L.
Torre : illustrated by Carol Inouye.
            p.    cm.
      "Adapted from The pearl that shone by night, in Favorite
folktales of China."
      Summary: Two brothers go on a quest for a luminous pearl
in order to win the Dragon King's beautiful daughter for a wife.
      ISBN 0-531-05890-5. — ISBN 0-531-08490-6 (lib. bdg.)
      [1. Folklore—China.]    I. Inouye, Carol, ill.    II. Title
PZ8.1.T6214Lu    1990
398.21—dc20                                         89-70999
[E]                                                      CIP
                                                          AC

To Jason, Sean, and Alexandra

Long ago in the Eastern Sea there lived a Dragon King
and his lovely dark-haired daughter Princess Mai Li,
who was as intelligent as she was beautiful.

Now that his daughter had reached a marriageable age,
the Dragon King was trying to find a suitable husband for her.
He introduced her to one prominent suitor after another.

One was too tall.

One was too fat.

One was too pompous.

One was too lazy.

To his dismay, none of his choices
met with her approval.

Exasperated, the Dragon King demanded of his
daughter one morning, "What kind of husband
do you want?"

"Father," Princess Mai Li replied, "I am not
looking for a man with money or position.
I want a man who is honest
and brave."

Now that the Dragon King knew exactly what she wanted, he thought it would be an easy task to find her a husband. But alas . . .

Prime Minister Tortoise recommended one, but he was not to her liking.

Senator Crab suggested another, but he also failed to win her approval.

Governor Porpoise knew a perfect candidate, but the determined Princess did not agree.

The Princess fretted and waited impatiently.

Finally Admiral C. Horse, who had just returned from a river inspection tour, told her about a young man who lived on a river bend at the foot of the mountain. Although very poor, he was known far and wide for his honesty and bravery.

As she listened, the Princess smiled with delight, but the Dragon King frowned. "How can we be sure that he is truly honest and brave?"

The eager Princess would not rest until General Octopus came up with a plan to test the young man. When the King heard it, his face lit with pleasure.

That very night the honest and brave young man
Wa Jing dreamed that a beautiful dark-haired maiden was
waiting for him on the bank at the bend in the river.
He woke up excitedly and told his older brother We Ling,
who listened with great envy.

His older brother quickly said, "It's just a dream.
Don't be foolish. Go back to sleep."

But soon as Wa Jing fell asleep, his older brother
stealthily dressed and hurried to the bend in the river.

The same dream woke the younger brother Wa Jing up again.
The lovely girl in the dream haunted his thoughts. Quickly he
threw on his clothes and rushed to the bend in the river.

He found his brother there. His angry words were
stopped by the magnificent sight before his eyes.

A full moon hung high in the sky, and a gentle breeze was blowing. Silver moonbeams were glittering on the surface of the river while fireflies flew back and forth— each carrying a tiny lantern.

And just as in the dream, there on a rock at the bend in the river sat the beautiful Princess Mai Li, her long black hair trailing in the river.

Both brothers immediately wanted to marry her.

Casting a sidelong glance at them, Princess Mai Li thought them very much alike, but somehow very different. Aloud she said, "Whom shall I choose? Tell me, which of you is honest and brave?"

"I am!" replied both brothers together.

"Very well," the Princess vowed. "Whichever one of you can

bring me a luminous pearl that shines
in the night will become my husband."

"But where is such a pearl to be found?" they both asked.

"It is in the keeping of the Dragon King of the Eastern
Sea," she explained.

Princess Mai Li then handed
each of the brothers a magic
water-cleaving scythe and
promised, "This will make a
passageway for you in the
Eastern Sea."

"Where is it?"

"How far away is it?"

To each question she answered,
"You must find it yourself."

The older brother We Ling rushed away to begin his search immediately, while the younger brother Wa Jing lingered with the beautiful Princess Mai Li, falling more and more in love with her.

When Wa Jing returned to the hut, he found that his brother had taken all their valuables, all their food, and their one horse.

So Wa Jing took his knapsack and began walking quickly down a little path along the river. Each brother in his own way journeyed for many days, starting at dawn and stopping at dusk.

The older brother arrived first at a village which had been devastated by a flood. Houses were under water. Fields were water-logged. The old folk, women, and children had taken refuge on the mountainside while the young men were trying to recover the belongings of the villagers.

The people were beginning to panic. They knew that if the water did not soon recede, the crops would perish and the houses would collapse.

We Ling, who had just finished his last morsel of rice cake, overheard them talking. "Who will go to the Dragon King and borrow his Golden Dipper? That's the only thing that will save our village."

"I'm on my way to see the Dragon King!" We Ling shouted. "I'll borrow the Golden Dipper for you if you will give me some rice." His offer brought forth a great cheer, since the villagers were frightened of the journey to the Dragon King. They quickly pooled all their food and gave it to We Ling along with a small boat to carry him across the river.

Later the younger brother Wa Jing, who had been living on wild berries and nuts, arrived at the flooded village. Seeing the havoc caused by the flood, he immediately began to help the young men, who were still trying to save the villagers' possessions.

When they told him about the Dragon King and the Golden Dipper that could save the village, he said, "I'm going to see the Dragon King. Why don't you let me borrow the Golden Dipper for you?" The villagers were puzzled to hear that another man was going to visit the Dragon King, but since he seemed an honest, helpful fellow, they put the matter into his hands.

Politely declining the villagers' last boat, Wa Jing dived into the river and swam across to the other side. He immediately set out for the Eastern Sea. When he reached its shore, he found his brother huddled fearfully there.

The Eastern Sea was like a vast battlefield. The wind sounded like blood-curdling howls, and the waves looked like thousands of cavalry soldiers charging onto the shore, effortlessly sweeping huge rocks into the sea.

Without the slightest hesitation, Wa Jing hurled himself into the waves, holding before him the magic scythe given to him by the beautiful Princess Mai Li. The water receded instantly on both sides of him. With his eyes squeezed tightly shut, the older brother We Ling followed his younger brother down the wide passageway to the bottom of the sea.

Soon they arrived at the gate of the Dragon King's golden palace. They were immediately taken to meet him. Upon hearing of their errand, the Dragon King took them to his treasure house.

Smiling secretly, the Dragon King instructed them, "You may each take one thing from my treasure house." As he pointed his finger at the door it opened instantly.

An astonishing scene greeted their eyes. The room was a topsy-turvy jumble of color. Treasures of every size and kind were spread out on shelves.

The older brother We Ling chose the biggest pearl he could find. Its dazzling light filled the entire room. But this was not enough for him. Everything he saw, he wanted. Golden ingots. Jade scepters. Diamonds. Emeralds. Rubies. He tried to sneak treasures into his knapsack, but the watchful guard quickly hurried him out of the treasure house.

The younger brother Wa Jing also saw the huge luminous pearls. But remembering his promise to the villagers, he took the Golden Dipper instead. With his head bowed in sorrow over losing the beautiful Princess Mai Li, he left the treasure house. His brother had already left without him.

The Dragon King personally escorted Wa Jing to the border of his underwater kingdom.

When the older brother We Ling reached the flooded village where he had left his horse, the villagers shouted, "Where is the Golden Dipper?"

"The Dragon King refused to lend it to me," he lied. With these words he mounted his horse and galloped away.

When the younger brother Wa Jing arrived at the village, he called to the people on the mountainside, "Come down. I have brought the Golden Dipper to you."

Wa Jing began to bail out the water. With the first scoop of the dipper, the water inside the houses receded; with the second, the crops reappeared; and with the third, all the water on the lowlands vanished.

When the water disappeared, a large oyster was revealed. The villagers pried it open and found a huge black pearl inside.

Overjoyed, the villagers gave the pearl to Wa Jing as a token of their gratitude. Wa Jing thanked them and put it into the bag on his shoulder. Although he was heartbroken not to have found a luminous pearl for the Princess Mai Li, he was glad to have kept his word to the villagers.

When the older brother We Ling got home he found Princess Mai Li on the rock at the bend in the river. He took out his magnificent pearl and presented it to her with both of his hands.

Without betraying her feelings, Princess Mai Li said wisely, "Let us wait until tonight to judge whether the pearl is genuine or not. Keep it until then."

When the younger brother Wa Jing arrived home, he went to see the beautiful Princess Mai Li with bowed head. "Please forgive me. I have failed to obtain a luminous pearl for you."

"But what do you have in that knapsack?" asked Princess Mai Li gently.

"Just an ordinary black pearl," said the young man sadly, taking it out of the bag. The pearl was dull and ugly.

"Why even the rocks on this river bend are brighter than that!" sneered his brother.

"Let us wait until tonight to judge whether the pearl is genuine or not," Princess Mai Li repeated.

That evening the older brother We Ling smugly took out his pearl from the bag on his shoulder. As soon as he did so, he realized something was wrong. Its glow had completely disappeared! Wailing and moaning in despair, We Ling hurled the pearl in the dirt and stamped furiously on it.

The Princess turned hopefully toward the younger brother Wa Jing as he opened his bag and took out his pearl. It dazzled like a million stars, turning the night into the brightest day.

Joyfully, Princess Mai Li took the pearl from Wa Jing's hand and tossed it high up into the air. It shone with a blinding light.
The older brother closed his eyes to shield them from the glare.
When he opened them he was alone.

The beautiful Princess Mai Li and the honest and brave Wa Jing, dressed in splendid ancient wedding robes, were already in the Dragon King's golden palace at the bottom of the Eastern Sea where a merry celebration was taking place. The beaming Dragon King and his equally gleeful advisors had arranged a scrumptious wedding feast in their honor.